Cumbria Libraries

KT-151-618

THIS WALKER BOOK BELONGS TO:

_____

_____

_____

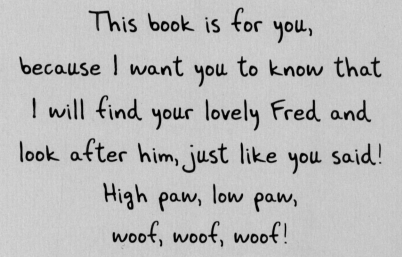
Grandpa's dog, Fred

Dear Grandpa,

This book is for you,
because I want you to know that
I will find your lovely Fred and
look after him, just like you said!
High paw, low paw,
woof, woof, woof!

Iggy x x

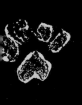

IGGY WILDER'S
GREAT
LOST
DOG
ADVENTURE

A STORY FOR DOG LOVERS EVERYWHERE

LOOK AT ME, IGGY WILDER

Hi, my name is Iggy Wilder. I may look like an ordinary boy, but I am not.
I have special dog powers! I can do most boy things, plus most dog things!
Which is barkingly brilliant because my Grandpa's dog, Fred,
has been sent away and I am going to find him.

He's a listener.

He's funny.

He's a hugger.

He's my mate.

Notice my sad face →

Q: Why is Iggy sad?
A: His not-so-lovely, parents have sent his Grandpa's dog, Fred, away to be REHOMED.

Unloved, empty, bare, hollow, vacant, uninhabited!

A SAD KENNEL

↑ This is Fred — the best, most missed Collie dog in the world!

This is a happy me — I will look like this when I find Fred!

Poor Iggy. Poor Fred.

4

Q: Why is a boy with dog powers writing a book?
A: Just because he's mad about dogs.

THE BOY WITH AMAZING DOG POWERS!

I am going to use all of my incredible powers to find Fred:

SCENTING

DIGGING

LEAPING

ROLLING

SHREDDING

BARKING

BEGGING

Q: Which of these dog powers will be the one to find Fred?

A: No dog knows. It might even be one of my hidden powers!

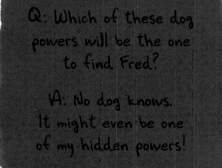

LYING DOGGO

My Grandpa used to say that Fred's canine talents had rubbed off on me because we played together so much. Now I can use those talents to find him. And I will find him ... oh yes, I woofing will!

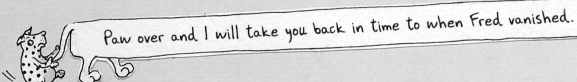
Paw over and I will take you back in time to when Fred vanished.

FRED WILL BE PINING FOR ME

He won't smile.

He won't play.

He won't eat.

His heart will ache.

A SAD DAY FOR ME AND A SAD DAY FOR FRED!

Poor me! → ← Poor him!

A dog would never "rehome" a pack member.

A dog remains faithful to its pack for life!

1. Most of my pack, or family as they like to be called, is indifferent to dogs – the one exception was my Grandpa Arthur. He loved dogs as much as I do, but he died a while ago. Before he died, he asked me to look after his dog, Fred.

You trust Iggy don't you, boy?
Whimper.

2. Well, you won't woofing believe this, but a week after Grandpa died I went back to school – brave boy that I am – leaving Fred on my bed.

Woof! See you later.

3. When I got home from school ... no Fred. My loved and trusted mum and dad had REHOMED him! They said that a son with canine powers was all the dog they needed in their family.

No sane family has TWO dogs!

4. I explained that Fred needed to be with his pack or he'd pine and die. Did they listen? No, they never listen to me, because they think I'm barking mad!

You're not listening!

5. I promised to pay for Fred's food with MY VERY OWN pocket money and walk him EVERY day. They still took no notice. Grrrrrr... My Grandpa asked me to look after Fred AND SO I WOOFING WELL WILL ... ONLY FIRST I'VE GOT TO FIND HIM!

I'd rather be a dog than a parent!

Sad dogs!

The trouble is Grandpa was my only doggy friend. The rest of my pack is totally lacking in canine understanding. So even if I find Fred, it's not going to be easy to persuade them to let him come home.

Dogs are best!

Pad back to the present and you will see what I mean.

Don't look!

I DO LOVE THEM... →

DRY-NOSED AND PAWLESS!

←SOMETIMES!

↑ This is my one and only GOLD DOGSTAR – awarded for being good. I am going to stick them all in this book, so that I can keep a record and then Mum and Dad can't cheat!

Sky, my sister, is an excellent storyteller. She collects notebooks but not the ones with dogs on the cover!

Emily, my mum, is a baby-minder and mad about babies and babies and more babies.

Roger, my dad, is a builder and very good with bricks, but not very good with dogs.

No, sorry, you've only got 49.

But I have proof!

By the way: those babies are not part of my pack – they go home at night!

Barbs, my grandma, was nice once – then Grandpa died and she turned grumpy. Even she doesn't want Fred to come home.

Groundling, the cat, smells of fish and drives me woofing wild!

A BOY WITH CANINE POWERS IS ALWAYS ONE PAW AHEAD OF HIS PARENTS!

Mum and Dad say that if I can collect fifty gold dogstars for being good, they will THINK about letting Fred live with us. They've only awarded me one gold dogstar before now – collecting fifty is going to require doggy determination.

Luckily for me and for Fred, I do have one very special friend who not only has a wet nose, but is often wet all over! So cross your paws, flip the page and let me introduce her.

Yes, dogs are best!

DAISY CLOUD
AND HER WATERY POWERS!

Good
at sports!

Good
at fishing!

Good at
retrieving!

Perfect
companions!

Woof!

This is my best mate, Daisy. She has canine powers too and has barked her promise to help me find Fred and collect gold dogstars.

We think Daisy got her canine powers from her aunt's dog. He's a water spaniel and Daisy's powers are definitely watery!

It's dogged, as does it — woof, woof, woof!

Daisy can nose out a puddle and splash and shake the contents for miles!

We are a dogged duo and together we'll use our powers to find Fred.

No dogstars today, surprise, woofing surprise. Probably due to my bathroom demonstration of Daisy's splashing skills!

Iggy, STOP!

I'm a water spaniel.

You're a mutt.

8

Tomorrow is another day and we are going to write a plan of action!

ACTION PLAN FOR FINDING FRED

1. COLLECT FIFTY GOLD DOGSTARS!

Daisy is going to train me to be good,
so that Mum and Dad award me
three dogstars every day!

(It would be a lot easier if I could award myself the dogstars!)

Daisy is nearly always good so she is going to train me how NOT to:

Kiss!

Chase the cat

Nice wall!

Knock down walls

Chew my cuffs

Eat Gran's biscuits

2. USE MY DOG POWERS!

Mustard?
SMELLS
Good dog!

We are going to perfect our dog powers
so that we never miss a scent or
a clue that might lead to Fred.

My cookpot awaits you!
Baaaaarmy!

We're going to be collies
and do our best
to round up Fred.

The best grandpa in the universe!
I'll woof to that!

Grandpa used to tell me a story about
Barry, a rescue dog. I've decided I'm going
to be as brave and clever as him!

Bother and growl, Daisy thinks we might find a clue to finding Fred in
Barry's story, which — yelp, yelp — means I've got to write it out for her.
Ok, paw over and let's see if the TALE OF BARRY guides us to the TAIL OF FRED.

Good at herding!

I've heard that before!

Easily bored!

Good at staring!

I'll woof to that!

Hairy perfection!

Mutts are best.

Mutts are perfect.

Barry (1800-1815)
Berne Museum, Switzerland.

1. A long time ago, many people tried to walk across the Great St Bernard Pass in the Alps. It was really dangerous and some of them got buried under the snow. So a monk trained St Bernard dogs to find them and dig them out.

2. One dog, Barry, was a real champion! He could scent a man under the deepest snow. Once he'd dug a casualty out, he'd keep them warm with his body and bark for the monks to carry them back to the monastery.

Where did these crumbs come from?

Yummy, they're biscuits!

They're evidence.

Dogs are always risking their lives for us! Some dogs are so barkingly brilliant at saving humans they are flown all over the world to help rescue victims of earthquakes and other disasters.

When I was little, Grandpa would pretend he was Barry rescuing me from a snowstorm. I do pine for my Grandpa.

ESCUE DOG!

Three woofs for Barry!

Monks opened the St Bernard's Pass hospice for travellers in 1050.

3. During one snowstorm, Barry scented a body trapped on a narrow ledge above a sheer drop. He bravely inched out onto the ledge, where a small boy lay half frozen to death. Barry started to lick his face and warm his body, until the child stirred and held out his arms to Barry.

4. Barry dragged the boy safely off the ledge. Sometime later, a monk heard him bark outside the monastery door and found him with the boy on his back. He would have frozen to death without the bravery and brilliant scenting skills of Barry!

Awarded for eating one carrot and two peas ... yuck! That makes 2!

Well, my Fred is going to pine to death without the bravery and brilliant scenting skills of yours truly, Iggy Canis Major Wilder (that's my full kennel name).

So tomorrow I'm going to see if I can pick up Fred's scent trail. Paw over the page and watch me sniff!

Brrrr! I've turned blue!

This page is freezing!

I told him not to chase the cat!

Luckily today's Sunday so I've had time to tune-in to Fred's scent.

I'm coming, Fred!

KEEP CALM AND CARRY ON!

Out onto the landing...

Woofily sorry, Sky!

down the stairs...

Back through the kitchen...

up the stairs...

HOW NOT TO COLLECT GOLD DOGSTARS!

Woofily sorry, Dad.

and straight into Dad!

BED!

Woofing cat!

Which is where the scent ended.

Mum and Dad did not award me a gold dogstar today — they sent me to bed early. I blame that Groundling for laying a false trail and tricking me into chasing her.

I have awarded Groundling a two-headed black cat with a forked tail ... the very worst! What's more, if she mews one more time, SHE'LL GET ANOTHER!

 **LATER**

I was dog tired but I had to call Daisy so I slunk downstairs to the telephone. Daisy said not to worry because she's got a new plan. She'll tell me about it at school tomorrow.

DAISY AND HER TOY DOG, NOBLE. He's half pug and has bloopy eyes!

Some toy dogs think they're real!

Well, I am real and that hurts!

14

THE END
OF A BAD DAY!

Snore, snuffle and yelp!

DAISY'S GREAT IDEA!

Daisy splashes or signs of a secret reader? Mmmmmm, interesting.

Daisy's new plan was fantastic. Together we have formed THE IGGY WILDER TRACKING CLUB to help us spot Fred's paw prints, fur trail and scent. We put posters up when we arrived at school today, so by breaktime we hope to have a whole pack of trackers!

THE IGGY WILDER TRACKING CLUB!
HELP FIND FRED!

DON'T DELAY!

JOIN TODAY!

BE ALERT FOR
↓
BLACK OR WHITE DOG HAIR
↓
PAW PRINTS
↓
HERDED SHEEP

BE DOUBLE ALERT FOR
↓
BURIED BONES
↓
SQUASHED GRASS
↓
THE CRY OF A PINING DOG

A SCRUFF-HAIRED COLLIE WITH A WAGGY TAIL

REWARD OF ONE YEAR'S POCKET MONEY WILL GO TO THE TRACKER WHO FINDS FRED.

Every member will receive special training and a badge.
Contact Iggy Wilder or Daisy Cloud at breaktime today!

I'm a computer genius!

BREAKTIME! Success! Our whole class has joined — except Rob, my neighbour and deadliest enemy. He teases me about my dog talents, becasuse he loves football and hates dogs! Now he's got nobody to play football with and is MAD with rage!

This is jawesome! Paw over for the next instalment...

Another gold dogstar! I ate all my supper without gobbling it straight from the bowl. I think that should be worth two, but that's parents for you!

I did try – really I did – only somehow I got tangled up with the ball.

Rob got the ball straight past me and into the net with one mighty kick ... the rat.

I got very cross with the ball... and burst it! Rob laughed of course.

My EX-club members laughed too. I hope they all have nightmares at his rotten sleepover.

Lobo

Mr Seton

So Rob made a fool of me and I've lost my trackers. Who needs them? I've got my dog powers ... and Daisy of course. The dogged duo will track you down, Fred, never you whimper. We will become as skilled as the wolf Lobo, who even tricked Mr Seton, the most famous wolf tracker of all time.

Look – a coffee mug ring! That's definitely not mine because I don't drink coffee and nor does Daisy.

Could it be a stranger?

Mmmm, sniff, sniff. I'm picking up a strange scent on this page. Someone is sneaking peeps at this book, I'm sure of it!

Could it be Mum?

Could it be Dad?

Mmmmmm, a grease mark too! Woofing weird!

Sorry, pet, but there it is.

No gold dogstars thanks to bursting the school football. I've got to pay for it out of my pocket money, which, as Mum kindly pointed out, means I won't be able to afford any dog food for Fred for quite some time. Mum can really make me growl! I'M GOING TO WRITE ABOUT LOBO AND MR SETON TO CHEER MYSELF UP.

BALL GAMES DOGS DON'T PLAY

Football

Cricket

Football

Football

Who's paying for our food?

Grandpa and I loved this wolf story – even though it is very, very sad.

My Grandpa had the heart of a wolf.

LOBO, THE WOLF KING, A

1. Lobo the wolf was nicknamed The King of the Currumpaw Valley. He lived and hunted in New Mexico with his small pack. Once he had hunted for wild animals but, over the years, ranchers had taken his land so now he raided their sheep and cattle. Many ranchers had tried to trap or shoot Lobo, but Lobo was far too clever for them.

2. At last, Mr Ernest Seton, the finest animal-tracker ever known, decided he would challenge Lobo. He carefully studied Lobo's habits before laying his most cunning traps. But even these were no match for Lobo. He scented them every time and even dragged some of the poisoned baits into a pile and pooed on them in scorn.

Mr Ernest Seton

My granny was a wolfhound. Shhhh.

18

MR SETON BECOMES A WOLF HERO!
After the death of Lobo, Mr Seton stopped killing animals and started to draw and write about them! He wrote a fantastic story about Lobo, which encouraged other Americans to respect their wolves instead of killing them. So although it was sad, Grandpa thought that if Lobo and Mr Seton hadn't met, American wolves might have become extinct.

Can you imagine a world without wolves?

3. Then, one terrible day, Mr Seton shot dead Lobo's beautiful mate, Blanca. All day Lobo's howls echoed around the valley as he called to her, but as evening fell and Blanca failed to answer, his howls grew sadder and sadder. In his unhappiness, Lobo grew careless and stepped on a trap that Mr Seton had scented with Blanca's blood.

4. When Mr Seton saw Lobo in his trap, he could not bring himself to shoot the great, proud wolf. Instead, he chained him up, gave him food and water and left him. Lobo stared out across the valley pining for his lost companion. The next morning, Mr Seton found Lobo lying dead and knew that he had died of a broken heart.

Normal wolf paw print, claw to heel: 11.5 cms

Lobo's paw print, claw to heel: 14 cms

Lobo was 90 cm high at the shoulder and weighed 68 kgs.

Today, wolves still have a struggle to survive, so I'm going to continue Mr Seton's fight to save them. Only right now I have a dog to find and I'm all of a quiver, because Lobo's howling for Blanca has given me a brilliant idea!

Don't delay, Paw over today!

GOLD DOGSTARS AT LAST! I've been so busy with Lobo that I haven't had time to get into trouble, so Mum has given me two gold dogstars! Hang in there, Fred, I'm making progress!

Don't mention wolfhounds here!

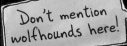

HOOOOOOWLING FOR FRED!

THE HOWL OF A WOLF

Wolves howl for bonding.

Wolves howl to stay in touch.

Wolves howl for lost friends.

DON'T DESPAIR THE DOGGED DUO ARE HERE!

It's nearly four months since Grandpa died and still no Fred. If I don't find him soon he might pine away and die like Lobo. So paws crossed that my grrreat plan works because I can't wait to stroke Fred's soft ears again.

No dogs allowed!

KEEP OUT

Today is Rob's sleepover. Daisy and I weren't invited but we have our own plan.

HELP FIND FRED

MISSING FIND FRED

We have to be good, or Daisy will be sent home, but we secretly put up some posters.

He's been rehomed!

Smelly mutt.

HELP FIND FRED

LATER Dad, Grandma and Sky spotted the posters and tore them down. Groundling smirked.

Grrrrrrrrrrrrrrrrrrrrrrr!

NO BITING!

I wanted to nip them, but I chewed my cuff instead. I hope Mum doesn't find out!

Are you hungry?

Starving!

To keep out of trouble, we're going to bed early. We're starving but we won't eat Grandma's biscuits!

We'll just have one each, or maybe two...

Or three, or four, or any number!

Well, we weren't going to eat Grandma's biscuits, but then WE DID!

I wish I had a bed.

Look! A thumbprint... someone IS reading my book.

My alarm is set for midnight because, as all wolves know, howls travel further on the still night air!

Kids howl in anger.

Kids howl in sorrow.

Kids howl when they're lost.

As soon as my alarm went off, Daisy and I crept outside into my garden den.
There we began to HOWL FOR FRED –
just like wolves howl for a lost pack member!
Tense with excitement, we listened for Fred's answering howl.

Nah, nah! We told on you. Nah, nah!

We had just caught a sound on the wind
when two parental arms grabbed us.

Dogs are bad enough.

We are the champions!

But wolves take the biscuit!

Tale-telling ROB had called our parents!
Daisy and I were in BIG trouble.

At least Grandpa's photograph still smiled at me as
I crawled into bed. I'm sure I heard Fred's answering call
just before Dad grabbed me.

I award Rob two black two-headed cats with forked tails!

I also award myself five dogstars for effort. I know Mum won't count them, but I think I deserve them just the same.

Snore, Mum.

A dog never tells tales.

21

DOGS ARE SO COOL!

CANINE POWERS CAN'

They can't whisper!

Dogs don't whisper behind backs.

Only sometimes!

Dogs don't exclude anyone.

It's tempting!

Dogs don't rehome pack members.

What, they share?!

Dogs don't hog the tasty titbit.

"When he was a baby he'd lick my nose instead of kissing me!"

"He's never wanted to build walls – just knock them down."

I woke up this morning and scented the air. My pack was in the kitchen whispering about me, so I slunk down stairs and hid under the table to listen. They have no intention of letting Fred come home, but I kept my mouth zipped until Grandma mentioned Grandpa ... that was too much!

Whispering unsettles my nerves.

Cover your ears.

GREY HAIRS!

Mmmmmm! More proof of a sneaky reader!

They must be mum's – she's always pulling out her grey hairs. I'm sticking them in as evidence!

DOGS ARE SO GREAT!

When Iggy was in his cot, a fairy flew in and sprinkled him with dog sparkles. I expected him to grow fur!

Did you say "purr"? Is he a cat now? You're too soft on him ... if only his Grandpa was still alive he'd soon put a stop to all this doggie nonsense!

I grabbed her foot in my canine jaw, tore off her slipper and ripped it to shreds! Grandpa LOVED me and my dog powers. What's more, he asked ME to look after FRED and I will! Everyone is talking about me, BUT NOBODY IS TALKING TO ME... It's a growler!

Good dog!

Dogs praise each other.

Hark, I hear a rabbit!

Dogs listen.

It's mine!

Dogs help each other.

GRRR GRRR

Dogs share the tasty titbits!

If only people were more like dogs, jawesome, jawesome dogs...

Ooooh, trouble

I DO LOVE DOGS

As I am still in the doghouse, without a friend in the world — not even Daisy — I've spent the last few days drawing dogs.

Good dogs

Little dogs

Sporting dogs

Fat dogs

Clever dogs

Big dogs

Kissing dogs

Slow dogs

Dancing dogs

Numerate dogs

Thin dogs

Upside-down dogs

O H Y E S I D O !

It cheers me up to think that there are so many woofingly wonderful dogs in the world ... including Fred!

Sad dogs

Courting dogs

Cross dogs

Naughty dogs

Juggling dogs

Hugging dogs

Listening dogs

Dogs are better at this than some people I know.

Puppy dogs

Gold dogstars (extremely rare)

A whole week has gone by and not one smile or gold dogstar! I'm so down that you might turn the page and find I've run away.

Talking dogs

Laughing dogs!

25

A NEW PLAN!

CANINE STAR!

OK, I'm still here, but only because it seems that Daisy hasn't forgotten me! She secretly sent me this advertisement:

Does your dog need a new home? Then contact THE DOG LADY: BOX 324. All breeds welcome.

Could Fred be with THE DOG LADY? Who is the Dog Lady? I'll have to give it some serious dog-thought.

DEAR IGGS, I thought Fred might be here ... but I don't know where "here" is. Shall we go hunting? HP, LP, W, W, W! Daisy.

LATER:

I've decided that Box 324 must be a kennel and that I will track it down. I can't risk taking Daisy because I might get lost. I shall leave at sunrise tomorrow...

My emergency tracking tools are packed.

| Biscuits | Magnifying glass | More biscuits | Tweezers | More biscuits |

(These biscuits are from MY secret supply, not Grandma's!)

Very important... If I get lost the following pages may be blank... In this case, please give this book to Daisy Cloud and ask her to howl for me! Goodnight and good barking! Am I scared? What, a boy with my canine talents ... no chance!

I'm full to bursting!

Zzzzzzzz

I have just done a gold dogstar count and things are looking bad. I can't bring myself to say how many I've got, but it's not woofing enough!

SHOCK AWAKENING!

It was still dark when I was woken by GRANDMA! Had she discovered my plan?

I was sure she'd come to rehome me. How would I search for Fred now?

In a flash I was down the stairs ...

out of the front door ...

and strapped into her bike trailer!

Then Grandma peddled off down the road at top pensioner speed ... zoooooooom! This was not part of my plan.

THIS WAS SCARY!!!!!!

I'm scared, wake up!

I thought it best not to try and imagine where we were going.

I hoped at least I would be rehomed with Fred.

On the other paw it didn't seem very likely.

I WONDER IF FRED FEELS LOST AND ALONE, JUST LIKE ME

Never trust a Granny.

No, I won't!

At last we came to a river, where Grandma stopped pedalling and started panting.

Time to escape... I clicked the latch, threw off the straps and jumped.

I landed, with a horrible bump and a splash, in a rowing boat ... and so did Grandma!

I growled in horror. I was about to be rehomed by my very own Grandma ... or was I?!

NO I WASN'T! You won't believe this but it was Grandma sneaking peeks at my book, and it had made her realize how upset Grandpa would be that Fred was living with strangers. We were off to FIND FRED ... together! I howled with happiness and SO DID GRANDMA!

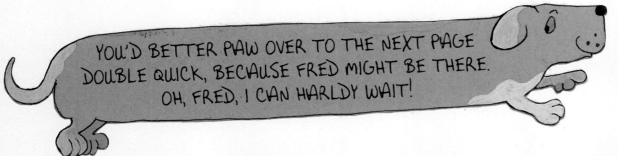

YOU'D BETTER PAW OVER TO THE NEXT PAGE DOUBLE QUICK, BECAUSE FRED MIGHT BE THERE. OH, FRED, I CAN HARLDY WAIT!

DOG SENSES

An hour to go.

Dogs sense when friends are close by.

Well, maybe two.

Even if the friend is slow.

They prepare themselves for ...

the mighty "welcome leap"!

Do you feel left out?

Grandma started to row, round and round and round and ... round in circles. Yelp! I had to act.

I told you I could row.

I focused my scenting powers and aimed the boat in the directon of a strong doggie whiff.

What now, pack leader?

324

My powers had not let me down – here was a sign with 324 on it, like in the advert.

Yelp!
Snuffle!
Yap!
Woof!
Bark!
Bark!
Woof!
Woof!
Snuffle!
Bark!
Yelp!
Woof!
Yap!

As we laid in the mud, the hedge erupted with a pack of wagging, yelping children and dogs. They scooped us up and herded us towards a farmhouse.

THIS IS SUCH AN EXCITING MOMENT!!!!!
Please note, I am smiling, but that cat is not!

THE DOG LADY AND HER PACK!

> Down, children, give him space!

DOG GREETINGS

Welcome!
Dogs always welcome you home.

Paw, paw!
It's polite.

It's bonding.

It's the best!

Outside the front door I saw somebody who could only be the DOG LADY, grinning like a Dalmatian! As she gave me a great doggy greeting, I noticed that there were dog heads poking out of every window. One of those heads <u>had</u> to be Fred's. So why, oh woofing why, couldn't I see him?

I COULDN'T SEE HIM BECAUSE HE WASN'T THERE.
IF YOU DON'T BELIEVE ME, SEARCH FOR YOURSELF!

Corners are lonely places.

Another egg... oh how delightful!

WHERE IS FRED?!

He missed you pet.

He kept howling.

As Grandma ate breakfast the Dog Lady told me that Dad had asked her to look after Fred, but Fred had run away. She thought he must be looking for me and hoped that now I was there, he'd pick up my scent and come back.

Let the lad find Fred.

NO!

I was NOT going home without Fred.

Iggy's right, Fred should be with us.

You're worse than a dog!

Mum cried and Dad told Grandma she should know better.

HOOOOO

I began to howl...

Wait... I'm coming, Fred!

I LEAPT out of the house.

I hopped across a field.

Moo!

I leap-frogged over a cow...

and over a hedge...

Grrrrrrrr!

OH, WHERE IS HE?

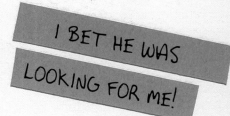

You're in BIG trouble!

Only just then, Mum and Dad burst in!

They had come to take me home – no chance!

OOOOOWL!

And the other kids joined in!

Hushhh!

Until the Dog Lady ordered us all to stop and listen.

Did you hear that?

I DID!

From far away I heard the answering howl of FRED!

Quack! Quack! Quack!

Woof, I must be a water spaniel!

I skipped over a river.

Hoooooooowl!

to an old pigsty!

It's SO exciting!

PUPPY FACTS!

They wee... a lot.

They chew... a lot!

They wag their tails ... a lot!

They play... a lot!

I peered through the door. There, in the gloom, was my Grandpa's Fred. Fred, eight pups and their mum, Lola... my heart went thump and I smiled and smiled!

Then Fred selected the cutest pup and took it outside to my Mum.

I hope Mum heard what Fred said as he gave her the pup.

Fred had rehomed himself with Lola, but he wanted me to have
A FRED AND LOLA PUP FOR MY BIRTHDAY!
I put my arms around Fred and squeezed him much too tight.
Mum said I could have the pup if I earned enough gold dogstars,
so I had to leave Fred and the pups and go home and be GOOD!

The morning of my birthday took an age to arrive, but I had been
SO GOOD that Mum awarded me twenty gold dogstars — which, added to my
other stars, is ENOUGH FOR A PUPPY (because puppies are much smaller than dogs)!
Daisy and I barked with excitement all the way to Fred's. THE DOG LADY
had organized a DOG SHOW for my birthday and it was JAWESOME!
Me and my pup were the stars and we won the gold cup.

I'm going
to join
the circus!

 I'm hoping some of Rascal's canine powers will rub off on me ... I might even grow a tail!

PUPPY BIRTHDAY!

We filled it with sparkles and sprinkled them over my pup while we
named him Rascal, because that was Grandpa's pet name for me.
I didn't want to go home, but I knew I would be visiting Fred again soon.
So I gave him a giant dog-hug and he gave Rascal a bit of a nuzzle ...
and me a top secret word of canine advice! Then I climbed in the car
with the rest of my pack, HUGGING MY VERY OWN PUP!

Bravo,
splendogorous!

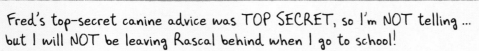

Fred's top-secret canine advice was TOP SECRET, so I'm NOT telling ...
but I will NOT be leaving Rascal behind when I go to school!

Rascal

Dear Grandpa,
I hope you can read this,
because I promised to look after
your Fred and I think you'll agree
that I've kept that promise. It hasn't
turned out quite how I imagined, but
I think that Fred is as happy now
as he could ever be without you ...
and that goes for me too!

High paw, low paw, woof, woof, woof!

Iggy (and his little Rascal).

First published as My Great Lost Dog Adventure, 2010
by Walker Books Ltd 87 Vauxhall Walk, London SE11 5HJ

This edition published 2011

2 4 6 8 10 9 7 5 3 1

© 2010 Marcia Williams

The right of Marcia Williams to be identified as author/illustrator of this work has been
asserted by her in accordance with the Copyright, Designs and Patents Act 1988

This book has been typeset in Bokka and GFY Palmer
Image credits: p10 photograph reproduced with the permission of the
Natural History Museum, Berne; p18, Mr Ernest Seton © 2010 MEPL

Every effort has been made to trace the ownership of all copyrighted material and
to secure the necessary permission to reprint the material used herein.
In the event of any question arising as to the use of any material, the publisher,
while expressing regret for any inadvertent error, will be happy
to make the correction in future printings.

Printed in China

All rights reserved. No part of this book may be reproduced, transmitted or stored
in an information retrieval system in any form or by any means, graphic, electronic
or mechanical, including photocopying, taping and recording, without prior
written permission from the publisher.

British Library Cataloguing in Publication Data:
a catalogue record for this book is available from the British Library

ISBN 978-1-4063-2997-1

www.marciawilliams.co.uk

www.walker.co.uk

WALKER BOOKS
AND SUBSIDIARIES

LONDON • BOSTON • SYDNEY • AUCKLAND

MARCIA WILLIAMS

With her distinctive cartoon-strip style, lively text and brilliant wit, Marcia Williams brings to life some of the world's all-time favourite stories and some colourful historical characters. Her hilarious retellings and clever observations will have children laughing out loud and coming back for more!

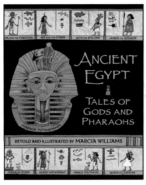

ISBN 978-1-4063-2668-0

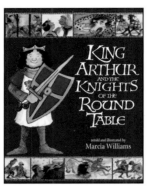

ISBN 978-1-4063-1866-1

ISBN 978-1-4063-2610-9

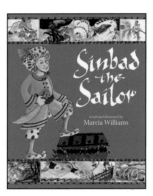

ISBN 978-1-4063-1944-6

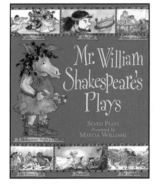

ISBN 978-1-4063-2334-4

ISBN 978-1-4063-2335-1

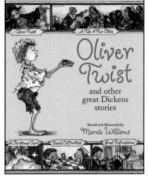

ISBN 978-1-4063-0563-0

ISBN 978-1-4063-0562-3

ISBN 978-1-4063-1137-2

ISBN 978-1-4063-0171-7

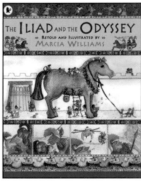

ISBN 978-1-4063-0348-3

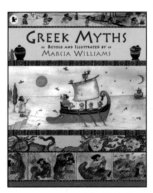

ISBN 978-1-4063-0347-6

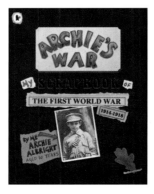

ISBN 978-1-4063-1002-3

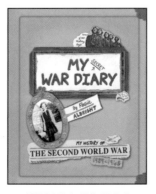

ISBN 978-1-4063-0940-9

AVAILABLE FROM ALL GOOD BOOKSTORES

www.walker.co.uk